The Trump administration started a secret vaccine program on animals in January.

The vaccine was a complete failure with one caveat. All the animals had an amazing side effect. The Males had an unusual growth in their genitalia. Donald immediately wanted a dose, his health officials informed him that it was not safe yet. The President always willing to make a profit put Ivanka in charge of marketing the drug and insisted on testing the drug on Steven Mnuchin and William Barr.

Viagra and Cialis strongly objected to the project.

Donald hired a publicist for the animals and thus created a high-priced getaway called,

"The Mysterious Island of Erectus"

Of course, you must sign a waiver in case your dick explodes

Hurry before Ivanka triples the price

Here is the first coloring book of 20 of the critters………

KONG KOCK

SKIPPY
DICKY
KANGA
RICKY

V.H.
RHINO
(VERY HORNY)

HENRY THE HORSE
DANCES THE
WALTZ

POLY-PENIS
FLAPPER

SAHARA SAND
CREEPER

WHALE
WONG

THE PROMISCUOUS WILDEBEEST

PAULIE THE 
BE STRONG
PENIS PACKED
PACHYDERM

COCKED BACK CHAMELEON

RUNNING BEAR
SHLONG

DOUBLE
RUDDERED
MANATEE

DICK HEAD
SPIDER

ZEBRAFIED PENIS

LAUGHING
PENIS
HYENA

STRAP
ON
ANT
EATER

SCREWY
DICKED
DUCKY

"GIRAFFE DICK" LOUIE

SLOTHY
THE UPSIDE DOWN
MASTERBATER

IGOR & VLAD
COCK & BLOOD SUCKERS